SHREK™

BEWARE OGRE

WRITTTEN BY
JUSTIN HEIMBERG

DESIGNED BY
LYNDA MODAFF

DreamWorks

For Shrek, bad hygiene was a source of pride. The ogre not only enjoyed being smelly and disgusting, but his body odor also drove away any unwelcome visitors who might stumble into his swamp. Ogres, and especially Shrek, like being alone.

Of course, it took work to be so gross. Every morning, Shrek followed a strict messiness routine. In the afternoon, however, he could take a relaxing dip in his swamp. He waded into the murky waters, squatted comfortably, and then carbonated the swamp with a huge burst of gas that sent any living creature floating to the surface.

Shrek's Morning Routine

8:00 A.M.: Mud Shower

9:00 A.M.: Brush Teeth
with Bug Guts

10:00 A.M.: Eyeball Breakfast

But Shrek's peaceful life was about to change. One evening, an angry mob of villagers from the neighboring land of DuLoc gathered on the edge of Shrek's swamp. They were hunting the ogre.

"All right, let's get it," said one villager.

"You can't just rush in there!" said another. "Do you have any idea what that thing will do to you?"

"Yeah," piped up a third villager. "It'll grind your bones for its bread."

"Actually, that would be a giant," said a helpful voice. The villagers turned to see who was correcting them. Standing behind them, his great green arms folded casually across his massive chest, was Shrek.

"Now, ogres...they'll shave your liver, squeeze the jelly from your eyes. Actually, it's quite good on toast!" Shrek smiled. Then, without warning, he gave a deafening roar, blasting spittle and bits of food into the villagers' terrified faces. By the time the roar's echo died, the villagers were gone.

Shrek wasn't the only one having trouble with the locals. All the fairy-tale folk in DuLoc were under siege. The ruler, Lord Farquaad, wanted to rid his land of magic creatures and relocate their fairy tails away from DuLoc. His soldiers were giving cash rewards for the capture of anyone magic.

In the front of a long line of villagers and their fairy-tale prisoners was an old woman with a donkey that she claimed could talk.

"That'll be ten shillings *if* you can prove it," said the skeptical guard.

The donkey, who wasn't stupid, stayed silent. Farquaad's soldiers didn't have time for this nonsense, so they seized the old woman and dragged her away. But she had fight in her brittle bones, and as she struggled, her foot kicked a birdcage that held Tinkerbell. *Poof!!* A cloud of fairy dust snowed down onto the donkey's hairy coat, and he slowly lifted off the ground like a balloon in a Thanksgiving Day parade.

"I can fly!" he exclaimed.

"He can talk!" said the guard.

"That's right, fool," said Donkey as he flew off toward the forest that bordered Shrek's swamp.

WANTED

PINOCCHIO

Possessed Puppet whose nose has been known to grow beyond the legal limit. Claims he is a real boy.

REWARD
300 Shillings

WANTED

EVIL FAIRIES
REWARD
25 shillings

WANTED
HUMPTY DUMPTY

REWARD
100 Shillings
Cracked-50 shillings
Sunny Side up-20 shillings
Scrambled-10 shillings

he fairy dust wore off, and Donkey hit the ground running. He galloped away from Farquaad's soldiers, going deep into the forest until he smacked into the smelliest tree trunk he had ever encountered. The tree trunk was Shrek's leg.

Now, few stay to chat with an ogre, so Shrek expected the donkey to scurry away in terror. The guards following him did. But Donkey was different. He not only wanted to come home with Shrek, he wanted to chat.

"I'll stick with you," he said. "Together we'll scare the spit out of anybody who crosses us."

This was too much friendliness for the ogre. He tried his favorite intimidation tactic: **AAAARRRRRrrr!!!!!** But Donkey wasn't intimidated. He just kept on talking.

Oh, WOW!

That was really scary. And, if you don't mind me saying—if that don't work, your breath certainly will get the job done. 'Cuz you definitely need some tic tacs or something 'cuz your breath stinks! Man!

9

Shrek lumbered back to his swamp, trying to ignore the blabbering donkey. When he reached his cottage, he ordered the chatterbox to stay outside. But Donkey wasn't the only one who now preferred the safety of the swamp to DuLoc... As Shrek sat down for his dinner, three blind mice interrupted his meal by knocking over his delicious supply of eyeballs. Then, seven dwarfs placed Snow White's glass coffin on Shrek's table. Even worse, the Big Bad Wolf, dressed up in a nightie, rested in Shrek's bed. And outside, on his precious private property, were a thousand fairy-tale refugees from DuLoc!

"What are you doing in my swamp!!!" roared Shrek.

"We were forced to come here," said Pinocchio, his legs shaking with fear.

One of the three little pigs added, "Lord Farquaad! He huffed, and he puffed, and he—signed an eviction notice."

Shrek was used to being alone. So the presence of three visually impaired rodents, a comatose princess with her posse of seven dwarfs, and countless other folk made this not-so-jolly green giant pretty d*%& mad. Lord Farquaad was going to hear a roar or two from Shrek, and if that didn't change his mind, then Donkey's endless chatter surely would!

The Three Bears

Goldilocks, try to get past our new alarm system!

The Big Bad Wolf

It's hard to be menacing while wearing a woman's nightie.

The Three Blind Mice

See how we sue! Animal rights activists are investigating our tales of abuse.

The Three Little Pigs
Our story really blows.

Meanwhile, in DuLoc, Lord Farquaad's Master of Interrogation brutally dunked the Gingerbread Man into a glass of milk. Farquaad himself mercilessly plucked at the cookie man's gumdrop buttons.

"No! Not my gumdrop buttons!" pleaded the desperate cookie.

"Who's hiding the rest of the fairy-tale trash?" demanded Farquaad. He was a tiny man, yet enormously cruel and vain.

But the cookie wouldn't crumble. He was spared only by the arrival of a new victim, the Magic Mirror.

"Mirror, mirror, on the wall, is this not the most perfect kingdom of them all?" Lord Farquaad inquired.

The Magic Mirror reflected. "Well, technically, you're not a king," it said.

Then the Magic Mirror showed Lord Farquaad three princesses and told him that by marrying one of them he would become a king, the King of DuLoc.

Farquaad chose Princess Fiona. But what about that dragon guarding her? His lordship wasn't going to break a nail fighting the beast. He'd find someone else to do it. He'd hold a tournament, and the champion would win the "honor" of rescuing the princess.

Bachelorette #1 is a mentally abused shut-in from a kingdom far, far away. Her hobbies include cooking and cleaning for her two evil stepsisters. Give it up for... **Cinderella.**

Bachelorette #2 is a cape-wearing girl from the land of fancy. Just kiss her dead, frozen lips and find out what a live wire she is.

Please welcome... **Snow White.**

Bachelorette #3 is a fiery redhead from a dragon-guarded castle surrounded by hot boiling lava. But don't let that cool you off. Yours for the rescuing... **Princess Fiona.**

Welcome to DuLoc

farquaad's tournament began the day Shrek and Donkey arrived in DuLoc City.

AWFULLY PERFECT, the many signs claimed. Perfectly awful, thought Shrek. He was repulsed by the city's cleanliness.

There was no one in sight, so the pair began to search the eerie, artificial town for Lord Farquaad. They hadn't gotten far when they heard a trumpet blast….

45 minute wait from here

Greeter
Giant Farquaad head terrifies children and keeps them in line.

You are here.

Souvenirs

Along with popcorn and candy, you can buy Lord Farquaad dolls, shirts, pins, mugs, posters, knee pads, and books on his life.

Welcome Booth

Animatronic dolls spout musical propaganda:
Welcome to DuLoc. Such a perfect town.
Here we have some rules, let us lay them down.
Don't make waves, stay in line
and we'll get along fine. DuLoc is a perfect place.

Souvenir photo of your first visit to DuLoc is complimentary.

Trams

Trams leave for "The Hassle at the Castle" at 1 P.M., 3 P.M., and 5 P.M. Watch knights sacrifice their lives for Lord Farquaad! No flash photography.

15

Shrek and Donkey followed the sound into a stadium where Farquaad's knights were assembled in front of a sellout crowd. The orderly rows of contestants parted in terror as the giant green ogre stepped onto the field.

"Knights!" commanded Lord Farquaad. "New plan. The one who kills the ogre will be named champion."

The knights charged Shrek with swords drawn. His only choice was to fight. Lord Farquaad watched as the surprisingly nimble Shrek knocked down each knight with moves worthy of a professional wrestler. Even Donkey took down a man or two.

"Congratulations, Ogre," Farquaad said as if he had planned this outcome. "You've won the honor of embarking on a great quest."

"I'm already on a quest," replied Shrek. "A quest to get my swamp back."

"All right, Ogre, I'll make you a deal," said the wily lord. "Rescue Princess Fiona for me, and I'll give you your swamp back."

Shrek had to agree.

The Ogre Vise:
Massive ogre hands apply pressure to the back of the opponent's skull; combination of restriction of blood flow to the brain and putrid stench from aired ogre armpits causes opponent to pass out.

16

The Donkey Punch:

The dirtiest move in the game. A swift kick that leaves a lucky horseshoe imprint for life.

Tombstone Pile Driver

Ye Olde Chair Shot

AIRPLANE SPIN

"I don't get it, Shrek," said Donkey as the pair left DuLoc City. "Why didn't you pull some of that ogre stuff? You know, grind his bones to make your bread?"

"For *your* information," answered Shrek, "there's a lot more to ogres than people think. Ogres are like"—Shrek glanced down at an onion he was snacking on—"onions. They both have layers."

Donkey thought for a moment. "You know, not everybody likes onions," he said helpfully. "Cake! Everybody likes cake! Cakes have layers."

Donkey, though he meant well, had missed Shrek's point. No one understood that ogres, like everyone else, are complicated. They aren't just big ugly monsters. They have feelings and dreams underneath their scary exterior.

Before long, the flowery fields of DuLoc gave way to a barren wasteland of dark jagged rocks. A pungent odor filled the air.

"Whew, Shrek!" gasped Donkey. "Did you do that? You gotta warn somebody before you just crack one off!"

"Believe me," Shrek snapped back, "if it was me, you'd be dead." He sniffed the air. "It's brimstone. We must be getting close to the Dragon's Keep."

And there it was: a burned and blackened castle, perched on a rocky pinnacle over a lake of molten lava. A single rickety bridge stretched over the boiling moat. Shrek walked onto the bridge, feeling it sag under his great weight, but Donkey froze.

"We'll tackle this together," assured Shrek. **"Just don't look down."**

"I'll handle the dragon. You go over there and find some stairs," ordered Shrek as they entered the dark, cavernous keep. "The princess will be up the stairs, in the tallest tower."

"What makes you think she'll be there?" Donkey asked, surprised by the ogre's sudden expertise in princesses.

"I read it in a book once," said Shrek.

ONCE UPON A TIME THERE WAS A LOVELY PRINCESS
yuck

SHE WAS locked away IN A CASTLE GUARDED BY A TERRIBLE FIRE BREATHING DRAGON

MANY BRAVE KNIGHTS had attempted to FREE HER FROM THIS DREADFUL PRISON
pathetic wimps

BUT NONE PREVAILED

SHE WAITED IN THE DRAGONS KEEP, IN THE HIGHEST ROOM OF THE TALLEST TOWER

FOR HER TRUE LOVE AND TRUE LOVE'S FIRST KISS
Wear helmet to avoid whole kissing issue

Donkey was glad he didn't have to look for the dragon. Stairs were scary enough for him. Unfortunately, ten steps down the dark corridor, Donkey found himself eyeball-to-eyeball with—**a massive red dragon!** He turned and fled, chased by a fireball of dragon breath. Shrek quickly shoved Donkey out of the fireball's blazing path. Donkey just kept running, with the dragon in pursuit.

"Gotcha!" Shrek shouted as he grabbed the beast's tail. But the dragon, with an easy flick, sent the ogre flying high into the air and right through the roof of the tallest tower.

Now the dragon could focus on poor Donkey.

Shrek crash-landed in Princess Fiona's bedchamber. There she lay peacefully asleep. Why do princesses seem to sleep so much? wondered Shrek. The Princess and the Pea, Snow White, Sleeping Beauty: all a bunch of royal sleepyheads.

"Are you Princess Fiona?" asked Shrek, attempting to wake her with a forceful shake.

"I am," she said as if she had rehearsed this line many times. "Awaiting a knight so bold as you to rescue me."

"Let's go," he said abruptly.

"But wait," pleaded Fiona. "This be-eth our first meeting. Should it not be a wonderful, romantic moment?" It was clear the princess thought the armor-clad ogre was her handsome prince.

"No time." Shrek grabbed Fiona by the arm and hauled her away as the dragon roared below. He had to rescue Donkey.

Dear Diary,

Slept late again. Looked out the window and pined for Prince. (Note: Getting really good at pining.) Did a nice cover version of "Someday My Prince Will Come" with more of an R & B sound. But it kept being interrupted by the screams of unfortunate adventurers who had stumbled upon the dragon. Being locked in a tower 24-7 can make a girl crazy. Woe is me. Woe is I, I should say (a princess can never be too precise with her grammar!). I am beginning to think my prince may never come, and I'll grow old alone in this tower.

Mrs. Prince Charming

25

Meanwhile, Donkey was having big problems. Big red-fire-breathing problems. He decided to do what he did best: talk. If he could befriend an ogre, maybe he could charm a dragon.

"Oh, what large white teeth you have. And do I detect a hint of minty freshness?" chattered smooth-talking Donkey. The dragon batted its long eyelashes, fanning Donkey. That's when he realized..."A girl dragon!" he said out loud. Donkey knew what to do. He would flirt his way out of danger—and right into the dragon's lair. Dragon clutched him in her coiled tail and breathed heart-shaped smoke rings in his startled face.

Just as the dragon pursed her lips and went in for a kiss, Shrek swung down on a candelabra chain and tried to grab Donkey. *THWUMP!* Shrek missed and instead received Dragon's wet one on his butt. He let go of the chain, and as it went up, the candelabra came down, landing like a collar around the dragon's neck. Shrek, Donkey, and Fiona made a run for it, with Dragon stuck like a dog on a leash.

PRECIOUS
OUR BABY

The lovelorn lizard struggled to follow her furry beloved, but was left to imagine what might have been . . .

How Does Your Man Compare?

Prince Charming   **Shrek**

❧ First Impression ❧

Sweeps you off your feet   Flings you onto his shoulder
                                        like a sack of yams

❧ Appearance ❧

Tall, dark, & handsome   Green, fat, & loathsome

❧ Companion ❧

Noble steed   Blabbering donkey

❧ Personality ❧

Strong, silent type   Strong, violent type

"You did it! You rescued me!" Fiona cheered after they made it back over the bridge and onto safe ground. Her fairy tale was coming true, after all.

Now it was time for the long-expected kiss, the one she had waited for all those years. The one she had practiced on her pillow so often. In her most imperious voice, the princess demanded that the knight take off his helmet. When at last he did so, Fiona just stared at him blankly. "You're…an ogre?" she asked, though it was obvious.

Shrek explained the situation to the disappointed princess. "I was sent to rescue you by Lord Farquaad. He's the one who wants to marry you."

"Well, then tell *him* to rescue me," she snapped.

"I'm a delivery boy, not a messenger boy," Shrek said as he flung the protesting princess over his shoulder and began the journey back to DuLoc.

Bloodnut the Flatulent
This ogre could knock men out with his potent stench.

Throwback
The only ogre to ever spit
over three wheat fields

Gerald the Pear-Shaped
An ogre who once ate 4,000
live fish to lower the level
of a river and keep it from
flooding an ogre village

Shrek, carrying Fiona over his shoulder, walked steadily for the rest of the day, determined to deliver Farquaad's bride as soon as possible.

Fiona had finally stopped fuming and was now chatting with Donkey. As the sun began to set, she suddenly asked, "Shouldn't we stop to make camp?"

Shrek ignored her until he was interrupted by a voice that seemed too loud and large for a princess: "I need to find somewhere to camp now!"

So they camped. Fiona, demanding privacy, hid herself in a nearby cave just as the sun disappeared.

Shrek and Donkey lay outside, gazing at a night sky full of stars.

"There's Bloodnut the Flatulent," Shrek explained, pointing to a constellation.

Donkey couldn't see the shape. **"Man, it ain't nothing but a bunch of little dots."**

Shrek was a little irritated. "Sometimes things are more than they appear," he said, thinking more about himself than the stars. Donkey may not have understood Shrek, but Fiona, listening from her cave, nodded in sympathy.

ack at his castle, Lord Farquaad lazed about in his luxurious bed, daydreaming about his bride-to-be with a little help from the Magic Mirror. The mirror once again showed Fiona's beautiful, smiling face. "Perfect," growled Farquaad.

Meanwhile, in the middle of an enchanted forest, the three travelers had encountered none other than Robin Hood. He gracefully leapt off a branch and swept Fiona high into a tree.

"I am your savior and I am rescuing you from this green beast," Hood said smoothly. He then jumped to the ground, drew his sword, and called out, "Oh, Merry Men!"

Shrek was outnumbered. But before the Merry Men could attack, Fiona swung into karate action.

"Hiyaaaah!" she cried. Within minutes, she had knocked out Robin and every merry man with a series of skillful backhands, flying kicks, and expert punches.

When she finished, Fiona simply smoothed out her dress, smiled, and continued on her way with Shrek and Donkey following in stunned silence.

Ogre skin is thick, so it was a while before anyone realized that Shrek had one of Robin Hood's arrows stuck in his meaty rump.

"Shrek's hurt! Shrek's hurt!" screamed Donkey, panicking, "He's gonna die. Does anyone know the Heimlich?"

Luckily, Fiona remained calm. She removed the arrow. And after that, Fiona and Shrek's feelings started to change. They spent the rest of the day doing nice things for each other. Fiona whipped up a cotton-candy-like treat for Shrek by wrapping insect-infested cobwebs around a stick. And Shrek returned her gift with one of his own: a frog he inflated into a balloon. They were no longer in a hurry to see Lord Farquaad.

They made camp that afternoon by an old mill outside DuLoc City. Shrek cooked up one of his specialties: weedrat, rotisserie style.

"This is delicious," said Fiona, wolfing down the rat with an appetite not fit for a princess.

As the princess and ogre gazed at each other, Donkey interrupted. "Man, isn't this romantic? Just look at that sunset," he said, oblivious to the look being shared by his two companions. That was Fiona's cue. With a quick *good-night*, she raced into the mill.

Donkey took a long look at Shrek. "I see what's going on," he said. "I'm an animal, and I got instincts. I know you two were digging each other. Just go in and tell her how you feel."

"There's nothing to tell," said Shrek. "She's a princess and I'm an ogre."

Owl-Brain Ball

Sprinkle owl brains with bloodworms. Place contents in mouth. Chew for 2 to 3 minutes. Remove from mouth. Let bake in sun for 5 days. Juggle. Eat.

Stuffed Possum Pops (on a stick)

Find 4 roadkilled possums. Stuff possum cavities with 2 teaspoons maggots, 1 ounce bird beaks, 2 tablespoons fish eyes, and loose change. Marinate in swamp for 2 hours. Shove tree branch into possum. Ready to serve.

Ant Sock

Grab handful of ants.
Put in sock.
Eat.

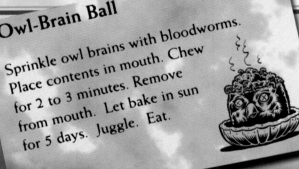

onkey decided to play matchmaker. He crept into the mill to talk to the princess, but the figure he saw in the shadows wasn't Fiona. It was an ogress! Donkey screamed.

"Shhhh! It's me. The princess!" hushed the ogress. "In this body!"

"Oh no! You ate the princess!" cried Donkey in horror.

"No," she explained. "When I was a little girl a witch cast a spell on me. Every night I become this horrible, ugly beast. That's why I have to marry Lord Farquaad tomorrow before the sun sets and he sees me like this. Only true love's first kiss can break the spell," she finished with a sob.

Donkey had calmed down now. "What if you don't marry Lord Farquaad?" he suggested. "What if you married Shrek?"

"Take a good look at me, Donkey," she said.

At that moment, Shrek had approached the mill door, holding a flower he'd picked for Fiona. He had decided to tell her how he felt, but he froze when he heard the princess speak. **"Who could ever love a beast so hideous and ugly?"** Shrek thought she was talking about him, and both his heart and the flower wilted at her words.

The next morning, Princess Fiona walked out of the old mill and saw Shrek stomping toward her.

"I've brought you a little something," he sneered. The little something was Lord Farquaad and his army.

Shrek took one last angry look at Fiona, snatched the deed to his swamp from Farquaad's hand, and stormed off.

The pint-size Prince Charming approached his beautiful bride-to-be. "Princess," Lord Farquaad said, after looking her over like a new car, "will you be the perfect bride for the perfect groom?"

Fiona shot an angry glance at Shrek's distant form. "Let's get married today."

Farquaad readily agreed. He and Fiona rode off together, and Donkey, with an anxious last look at Fiona, hurried after Shrek.

FROM THE DESK OF

Lord ƒarquaad

Perfect Wedding Planner

☐ On wedding cake, put extra icing under groom to make him look taller.

☐ Use Gingerbread Man for cake crust.

☑ Steal golden ring from lazy partridge in pear tree.

☑ Take Tom Thumb's platform shoes.

41

Safety Card for Dragon Airlines

Remain seated at all times. In the event of a crash, the person next to you may be used as a flotation device.

Exits are located all around you. In an emergency landing, flee, screaming like a baby, onto the wing until the dragon lands. In case of fire (and there will definitely be fire), stay on the dragon's good side.

If experiencing motion discomfort, lean over the side of the dragon and let loose. Because of wind resistance, don't face forward!

Back in his swamp, Shrek sat down for some fried weedrat in gerblecky. But, for the first time ever, he had no appetite. Suddenly, he heard a noise outside. It was Donkey.

"Back off," warned Shrek. He wasn't in the mood to see anyone.

But Donkey stood his ground. "You're so wrapped up in layers, onion boy, you're afraid of your own feelings. Just like with Fiona. All she ever did was like you. Maybe even love you."

That got Shrek's attention. "Love me? She said I was ugly! A hideous creature. I heard you talking."

"She wasn't talking about you! She…" Donkey stopped. He had promised to keep the princess's secret, but he'd said enough. Shrek knew he had to stop the wedding.

"We'll never make it in time," he groaned.

Donkey whistled, and Dragon appeared, hovering overhead like a rescue helicopter.

"I guess it's just my animal magnetism," said Donkey with a wink.

By night one way, by day another.
Until you find true love's first kiss.
And then takes love's true form.

A s Dragon soared toward DuLoc City, the wedding ceremony had already begun.

Fiona glanced nervously at the window, where the sun was dropping toward the horizon. "Could we just skip ahead to the end?" she asked.

The priest complied and made it official. There was only one thing left to do: Farquaad stood on his tiptoes to kiss Fiona.

Just then, Shrek burst through the cathedral doors. "I object!" he roared. "You can't marry him, Fiona. He's just marrying you to be king." He charged up to the altar.

"He's not your true love," said Shrek, looking deeply into Fiona's eyes.

Lord Farquaad laughed. "This is precious! The ogre has fallen in love with the princess."

"Is this true?" Fiona stepped forward.

At that moment, the sun set. A sudden burst of light and clouds of smoke shrouded Fiona. She began to transform. When the smoke finally cleared, a plump green ogress stood in her place. Farquaad's eyes grew wide with revulsion. The wedding guests gasped in horror.

"Well, that explains a lot," said Shrek.

"This marriage is binding!" cried Farquaad. "I am still king." He placed the royal crown on top of his head. "And as king, I order you knights to kill the ogre. And you, Princess…" Farquaad grabbed the ogress.

"I'll have you locked up in that tower for the rest of your life."

Farquaad's men surrounded Shrek. He knocked several to the ground before they managed to hold him. Still struggling, he gave a piercing whistle and Dragon came crashing through the window behind the altar. She swallowed Lord Farquaad in one great gulp.

"Nobody move," threatened Donkey from his seat on her head. **"I've got a dragon and I'm not afraid to use it."** Dragon belched and out rolled Farquaad's crown.

Shrek turned to his new Fiona. "Fiona," he said—this time he wasn't going to chicken out—"I love you."

"I love you, too," Fiona said.

Fiona and Shrek kissed. Then the ogress began to lift into the air and was once again shrouded in flashing light.

Finally, Fiona fell to the floor. The crowd waited in suspense to discover what love's true form would be. When Fiona rose again…she was still an ogress.

She felt her face. "I don't understand. I'm supposed to be beautiful."

"But you are beautiful," said Shrek.

Ogre and ogress joined hands in smelly matrimony as DuLocians and fairy-tale creatures watched happily. Fiona hurled her bridal bouquet into the crowd where Sleeping Beauty and Snow White battled over the prize. But sly Dragon quickly snatched the flowers in her snout, glancing at Donkey with a smile.

With a wave of her wand, a fairy godmother transformed a wild onion into a majestic carriage. The newlyweds hopped into their layered coach, waving to the crowd as they rode off into the sunset.

And they lived together, ugly ever after.

"God bless us, everyone."